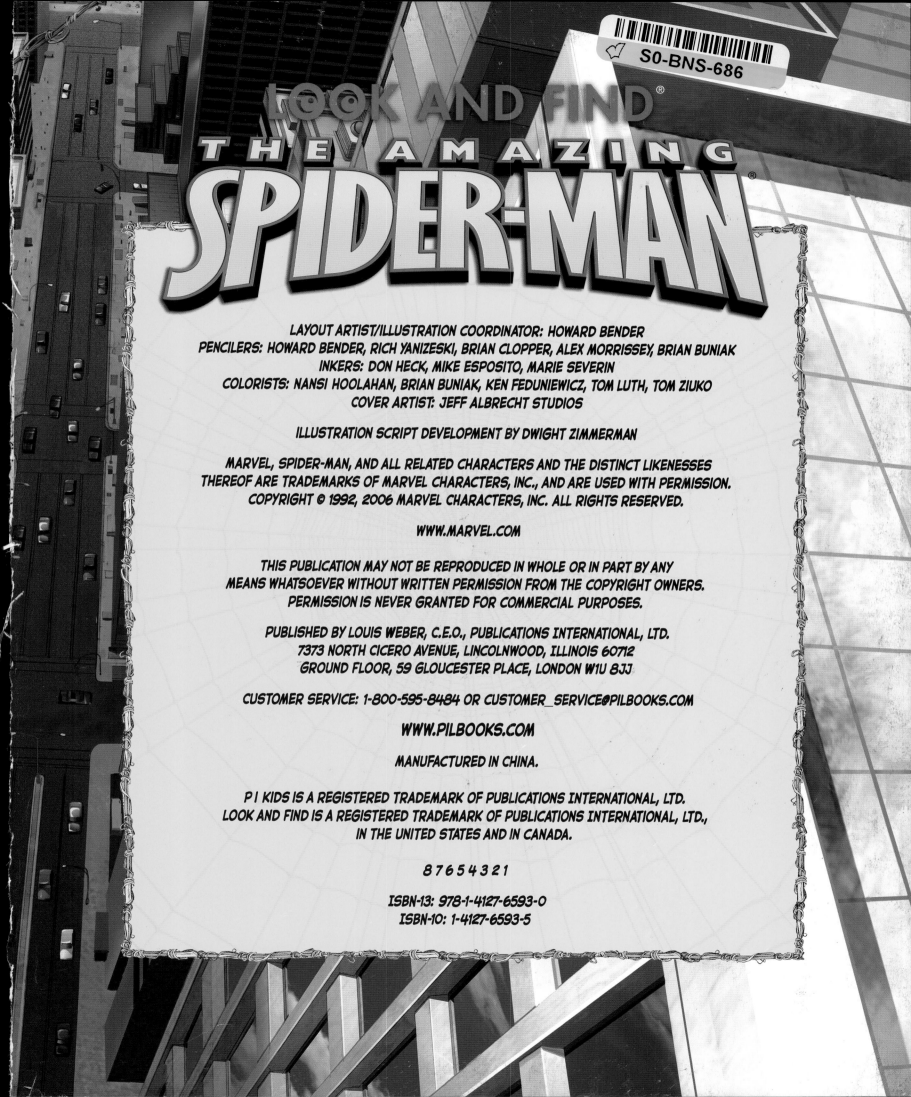

LOOK AND FIND®
THE AMAZING SPIDER-MAN®

LAYOUT ARTIST/ILLUSTRATION COORDINATOR: HOWARD BENDER
PENCILERS: HOWARD BENDER, RICH YANIZESKI, BRIAN CLOPPER, ALEX MORRISSEY, BRIAN BUNIAK
INKERS: DON HECK, MIKE ESPOSITO, MARIE SEVERIN
COLORISTS: NANSI HOOLAHAN, BRIAN BUNIAK, KEN FEDUNIEWICZ, TOM LUTH, TOM ZIUKO
COVER ARTIST: JEFF ALBRECHT STUDIOS

ILLUSTRATION SCRIPT DEVELOPMENT BY DWIGHT ZIMMERMAN

PUBLISHED BY LOUIS WEBER, C.E.O., PUBLICATIONS INTERNATIONAL, LTD.
7373 NORTH CICERO AVENUE, LINCOLNWOOD, ILLINOIS 60712
GROUND FLOOR, 59 GLOUCESTER PLACE, LONDON W1U 8JJ

CUSTOMER SERVICE: 1-800-595-8484 OR CUSTOMER_SERVICE@PILBOOKS.COM

WWW.PILBOOKS.COM

MANUFACTURED IN CHINA.

8 7 6 5 4 3 2 1

ISBN-13: 978-1-4127-6593-0
ISBN-10: 1-4127-6593-5

S0-BNS-686

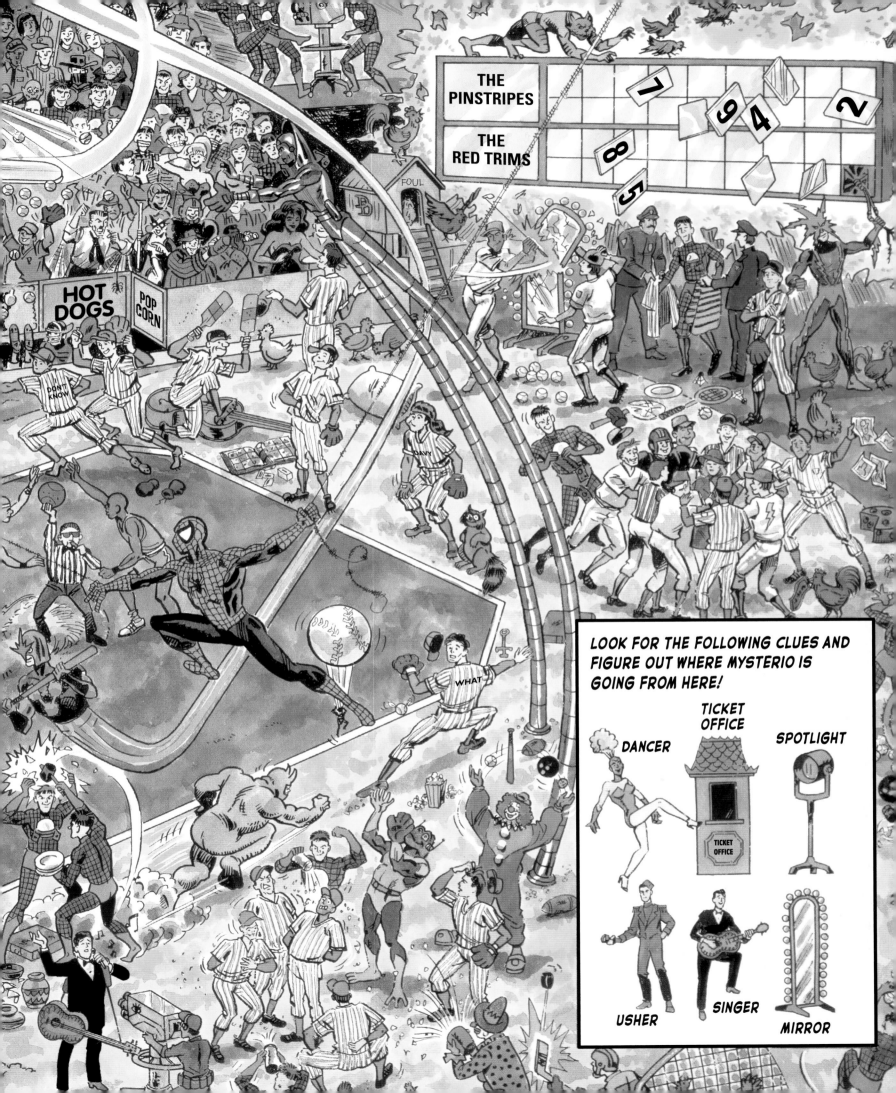

WHILE SPIDEY'S WORKING ON HIS PLAN, SEE IF YOU CAN FIND THESE THINGS THAT TELL WHERE MYSTERIO WILL GO FROM HERE.

THEATER MASKS

OPERA GLASSES

LION

ACTOR

ACTRESS

COWBOY WITH LASSO

I SHOULD HAVE GUESSED THAT MYSTERIO WOULD END UP IN THE TIMES SQUARE THEATER DISTRICT. HE PROBABLY FEELS RIGHT AT HOME HERE. IF ONLY I CAN SLIP A SPIDER TRACER ON HIM. THEN I'LL BE ABLE TO FOLLOW HIM ANYWHERE — EVEN TO HIS SECRET HIDEOUT.

IF SPIDEY CAN FIND THESE ITEMS, HE'LL HAVE AN IDEA WHERE TO GO FROM HERE. SEE IF YOU CAN FIND THEM AND FIND THE REAL SPIDEY, TOO!

TYPEWRITER
TELEPHONE
CAMERA
PENCIL & NOTEPAD
TAPE RECORDER
NEWSPAPER

I HAD TO CALL IN A LOT OF DEBTS, BUT I'VE GOT SOME OLD FRIENDS HELPING ME OUT NOW. EVEN AFTER WE GET ALL THESE BAD GUYS UNDER CONTROL, THE WORK WON'T BE DONE. MYSTERIO HAS PLANTED EIGHT BOMBS IN THE CITY STREETS. WE HAVE TO FIND THEM, OR THERE'S NO TELLING HOW MANY PEOPLE WILL BE HURT!

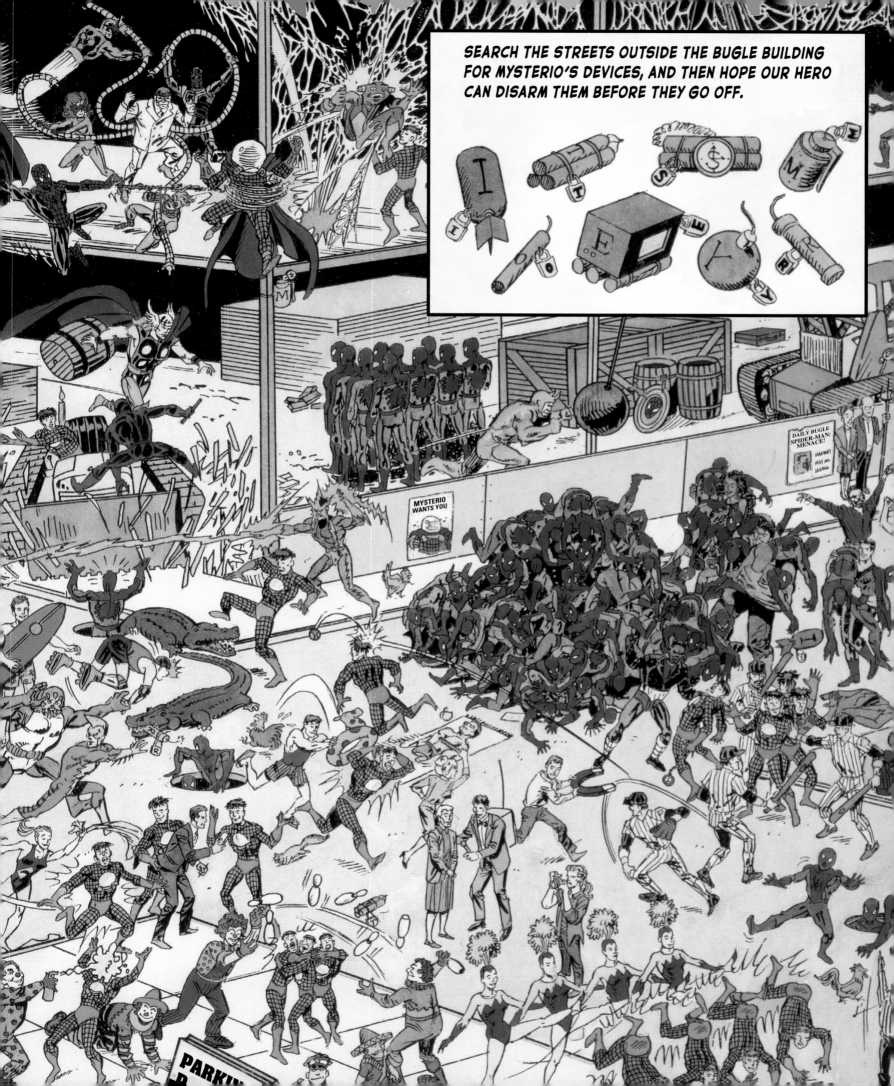

SEARCH THE STREETS OUTSIDE THE BUGLE BUILDING FOR MYSTERIO'S DEVICES, AND THEN HOPE OUR HERO CAN DISARM THEM BEFORE THEY GO OFF.

IN ALL THE CONFUSION BACK AT THE DAILY BUGLE OFFICE, PETER PARKER LEFT SOME THINGS BEHIND. SEE IF YOU CAN FIND THEM FOR HIM.

- [ ] A SPIDER-MAN MASK
- [ ] A SPIDER-MAN SHIRT
- [ ] SPIDER-MAN TIGHTS
- [ ] SPIDER-MAN GLOVES
- [ ] SPIDER-MAN BOOTS
- [ ] SPIDER-MAN WEB SHOOTERS
- [ ] A CAMERA

THE MASTER OF ILLUSION AND SPECIAL EFFECTS HAS MISPLACED SOME OF HIS GEAR. GO BACK TO THE BEACH AND FIND THESE THINGS MYSTERIO USED TO PLAY HIS TRICKS.

- [ ] A MAGIC WAND
- [ ] A DECK OF CARDS
- [ ] A TOP HAT
- [ ] A WHITE RABBIT
- [ ] A MAKEUP KIT
- [ ] A PAIR OF HANDCUFFS
- [ ] A FAKE MUSTACHE

THE SCARLET WITCH HAS LEFT SOME OF HER ITEMS OF SORCERY BACK AT THE AMUSEMENT PARK. HELP HER TRACK THEM DOWN BEFORE THEY FALL INTO THE WRONG HANDS.

- [ ] A WITCH'S HAT
- [ ] A BROOM
- [ ] A BLACK CAT
- [ ] A BOOK OF MAGIC SPELLS
- [ ] A FROG PRINCE
- [ ] A CANDLE
- [ ] TOADSTOOLS

MATT MURDOCK LIKES TO SPEND QUITE A LOT OF TIME AT THE BALLPARK. GO BACK THERE AND TRY TO FIND THESE DARING AND DEVILISH ITEMS.

- [ ] DAREDEVIL LOGO
- [ ] DAREDEVIL'S BATON
- [ ] A GRAPPLING HOOK
- [ ] A PAIR OF SUNGLASSES
- [ ] A PITCHFORK
- [ ] A PAIR OF BOXING GLOVES

ALL THIS CRIMINAL ACTIVITY IS MAKING FROG-MAN HUNGRY. HAVE A LOOK AROUND RADIO CITY MUSIC HALL FOR THESE SUCCULENT TREATS HE'D LOVE TO GOBBLE UP.

- [ ] A SPIDER
- [ ] A FLY
- [ ] A BEETLE
- [ ] A CATERPILLAR
- [ ] A BUTTERFLY
- [ ] A GRASSHOPPER
- [ ] A WORM

WHEN THE NORSE GOD OF THUNDER VISITS TIMES SQUARE, YOU'LL KNOW THAT HE'S BEEN THERE. SEE IF YOU CAN FIND THESE THINGS THOR MIGHT HAVE LEFT BEHIND.

- [ ] A JACKHAMMER
- [ ] A CLAW HAMMER
- [ ] A SLEDGEHAMMER
- [ ] A VIKING HELMET
- [ ] A MODEL VIKING SHIP
- [ ] A SWORD AND A SHIELD

THE BAD GUYS HAVE LEFT STUFF SCATTERED ALL OVER THE BUILDING THAT LEADS TO THEIR SECRET BASE. SEARCH THE SINISTER WAREHOUSE FOR THEIR VILLAINOUS POSSESSIONS.

- [ ] ANI-MEN'S DOGGIE BAG
- [ ] BIRD-MAN'S TAIL FEATHER
- [ ] CAT-MAN'S CLAW BOOTS
- [ ] FROG-MAN'S FLIPPERS
- [ ] APE-MAN'S FUR BRUSH
- [ ] MYSTERIO'S GLASS HELMET
- [ ] CALYPSO'S NECKLACE
- [ ] SANDMAN'S BUCKET AND SHOVEL

CALYPSO HAS MAGIC TALISMANS STREWN ABOUT THE SECRET HIDEOUT. RETURN TO THE CAVERN AND FIND THESE MAGICAL OBJECTS.

- [ ] A SKULL
- [ ] A SHRUNKEN HEAD
- [ ] A VOODOO DOLL
- [ ] A RAVEN
- [ ] A BONE
- [ ] A DAGGER
- [ ] A GOLDEN CUP
- [ ] A TOOTH NECKLACE

MYSTERIO MAY BE A MENACE TO SOCIETY, BUT SOMETIMES SPIDEY'S GREATEST ENEMY IS J. JONAH JAMESON. LOOK AROUND THE STREET OUTSIDE THE DAILY BUGLE FOR THESE THINGS THAT BELONG TO JJJ.

- [ ] A BOX OF CIGARS
- [ ] A SPIDER-MAN DART BOARD
- [ ] A BRIEFCASE
- [ ] A BUNDLE OF NEWSPAPERS
- [ ] A POCKET WATCH
- [ ] A SUIT COAT

SO YOU FOUND THE BOMBS THAT MYSTERIO PLANTED OUTSIDE THE DAILY BUGLE. GOOD WORK, BUT IF THEY AREN'T ALSO DISARMED, THE CITY WILL STILL BE DEVASTATED. LUCKILY, MYSTERIO HAS LEFT A WAY TO AVERT THE CATASTROPHE. EACH OF THE OTHER EIGHT PLACES HE VISITED HAS A HIDDEN KEY THAT WILL DEFUSE ONE OF THE BOMBS. GO BACK TO THE LOCATIONS, FIND THE KEYS, AND MATCH THEM WITH THE CORRECT BOMBS.